Lucy on the Ball

Lucy on the Ball

by Ilene Cooper
illustrated by David Merrell

A STEPPING STONE BOOK™
Random House New York

For Mary Frances Wilkens:
friend, colleague, and soccer mom extraordinaire.
And thanks to Keir Graff for his soccer expertise.
—I.C.

For my wonderful wife and our children
—D.M.

SteppingStonesBooks.com
www.randomhouse.com/kids

Educators and librarians, for a variety of teaching tools, visit us at
www.randomhouse.com/teachers

Library of Congress Cataloging-in-Publication Data
Cooper, Ilene.
Lucy on the ball / by Ilene Cooper ; illustrated by David Merrell. — 1st ed.
p. cm. — (Absolutely Lucy ; #4)
"A Stepping Stone book."
Summary: Lucy, the beagle, does not mind her humans very well until third-grader Bobby joins a soccer team, Lucy becomes the mascot, and the coach gives Lucy obedience training.
ISBN 978-0-375-85559-7 (pbk.) — ISBN 978-0-375-95559-4 (lib. bdg.) —
ISBN 978-0-375-89820-4 (ebook)
[1. Dogs—Training—Fiction. 2. Beagle (Dog breed)—Fiction.
3. Soccer—Fiction.] I. Merrell, David Webber, ill. II. Title.
PZ7.C7856Lor 2011 [Fic]—dc22 2010005183

Printed in the United States of America
10 9 8 7 6 5 4 3 2 1

Random House Children's Books supports the First Amendment and celebrates the right to read.

Contents

Soccer? Soccer!

Bobby Quinn put a few finishing touches on his drawing of his superhero. "Looks great, huh, Lucy?"

He didn't really expect an answer from Lucy, his pet beagle. She might be the smartest, cutest dog ever, but she couldn't talk. At least not yet.

Bobby was sprawled on the floor of his bedroom. Lucy was sprawled next to him.

Lucy was brown and white with a few black spots. Her brown eyes reminded Bobby of chocolate candy.

"This is Planet Man," Bobby informed Lucy. "He's absolutely the best superhero ever." "Absolutely" was one of Bobby's favorite words.

Planet Man had big muscles, feet like flippers, and hands like claws. He wore a bright yellow suit with PM on the front. Bobby was drawing Planet Man for art class. The assignment was to draw something about the environment. "Planet Man's job is to save the Earth," Bobby added.

Maybe Lucy couldn't speak, but she could bark. She barked a lot. She also liked to howl. She raised her head and glanced at Planet Man. *"Ho-o-wl."* Then she gave Bobby's arm a sloppy lick.

Bobby sat up and stretched. “Yep. You like Planet Man, too.”

Bobby had been on a roll lately. Things were absolutely going his way.

He used to be so shy he would barely look at people when he spoke to them. Thanks to Lucy, he had made new friends, some young, some old. He was having lots of fun now. The more fun he had, the less shy he was. He hadn’t even minded—too much—giving a report in front of his class.

“You’re sure a good girl,” Bobby said. He patted Lucy on the head.

“I wish that was always true.” Mrs. Quinn, Bobby’s mother, walked into his bedroom. She held a chewed-up slipper in her hand.

Bobby knew who was responsible. “Lucy!”

“I’m afraid she’s up to her old tricks,” Mrs. Quinn said with a sigh.

Lucy liked to chew things. She had gotten better for a while. But lately she seemed to remember how much she enjoyed tearing up shoes and socks—and slippers.

"We're going to have to do something about Lucy's chewing," Mrs. Quinn said.

Lucy gave another little howl. Then she got up and walked away. Both Bobby and his mother laughed.

"Well, I guess Lucy didn't think much of that idea," Mrs. Quinn said.

"Can I go over to Shawn's house?" Bobby asked. Shawn was one of Bobby's new friends. "I want to show him my drawing of Planet Man."

Mrs. Quinn nodded. She walked Bobby to the front door. "Don't be too long. It's almost time for lunch."

"Okay," Bobby said. He opened the door.

To his surprise, there stood Shawn. He was about to ring Bobby's doorbell.

"Hey, I was just coming to see you," Bobby told Shawn. He held up the picture of Planet Man.

Shawn didn't seem to notice it. Instead, he said, "We've got to get over to the park."

"Why?" Bobby asked.

"They're having sign-ups for the soccer league," Shawn explained. "It only goes until two o'clock, so we have to hurry."

"Soccer?" Bobby asked. He had never played soccer. He had never played any sport except T-ball.

Bobby liked to watch sports on television with his dad. He especially liked rooting for his favorite team, the Chicago Cubs. He wasn't very interested in playing sports, though. He didn't think he'd be very good.

"I played soccer before we moved here," Shawn told him happily. "My mom just found out that the park district has a soccer league. Let's go sign up."

Bobby glanced at his mother. His look said "Help!"

"Do you want to play soccer?" Mrs. Quinn asked him.

"I never thought about it," Bobby said.

"It's great!" Shawn told him. "Running up and down the field. Kicking the ball. Making goals."

Bobby wasn't sure he could see himself doing any of those things. Especially making goals.

"I don't know . . ." Bobby's voice trailed off.

Shawn looked disappointed. "C'mon, Bobby. I don't want to join a team by myself."

Like Bobby, Shawn was shy. And like

Bobby, he was getting less shy. Still, joining a team was a big deal. Bobby knew it was important to have a friend along for something like that.

Bobby's mother patted his shoulder. "It's good to try new things, Bobby."

"I guess so," he said uncertainly.

"Why don't I call your mother, Shawn, and find out more about the soccer league?" Mrs. Quinn asked. "That is, if you're sure about joining, Bobby."

He wasn't sure at all, but being on a soccer team with Shawn might be fun.

Shawn was waiting for an answer. So was his mother.

"All right," Bobby said slowly. "I'll try it." He put his drawing of Planet Man on the table in the hall. He would show it to Shawn later.

The rest of the afternoon passed by in a blur. First the boys went over to the big park in the middle of town. It was the park where Lucy had taken her obedience classes along with Butch, the laziest dog in the world. Butch's owner was also a new friend, a girl named Candy.

The park was full of noisy kids. Some of them stood in front of a few long tables. Several women from the park district were giving out permission forms. A lady with a name tag that said DEE handed one to Bobby. Dee told him his mother or father would have to sign it so he could play.

"Now I'll assign you to a team," Dee said.

A team already? Bobby thought nervously.

"Do you two want to play together?" Dee asked, looking at Bobby and Shawn over the tops of her glasses.

"Yes," they both answered.

"Okay, then, you'll be on the brown team. Mr. Morris is the coach." Dee pointed him out. "He's over there. You can say hello to him when we're done."

Mr. Morris was a big man. Tall and wide. His gray hair was short, in a crew cut. He was not smiling.

Bobby looked at Shawn. Shawn looked at Bobby. Maybe they would wait to meet Coach Morris.

"Here's a list of things you will need for soccer." Dee handed them each another sheet of paper. "You should have them all for the first practice. The date of the first practice is right there on the bottom of the page."

Bobby and Shawn thanked Dee. Then Bobby felt a hand on his shoulder. It was Candy. Candy liked to talk a lot, especially when she was excited. She was excited now.

"Hey, I didn't know you guys were trying out for soccer. Maybe we're on the same team. I'm on the brown team. My dad said boys and girls usually have their own teams. But I guess our town's too small for that. I hope my team has a lot of girls. Not that there's anything wrong with boys. I like you two and you're boys."

Bobby and Shawn laughed. "Yes, we know we're boys," Bobby said.

"And we're on the brown team, too," Shawn added.

"Great!" Candy said. "I can't wait to start kicking the ball around."

Candy pretended to be kicking an imaginary ball. Bobby noticed she could kick pretty high.

Shawn was smiling. He pretended to kick the ball right back at her.

It's good to try new things, Bobby reminded himself. That was what his mother had said.

He hoped she was right.

2

Big News

"Kick it to me, Bobby!" Shawn danced around his backyard.

Bobby and Shawn had been trying out Shawn's new soccer ball for the last half hour. And for the last half hour, Bobby had been trying to kick the ball to Shawn. Sometimes it went too far. Sometimes it didn't go far enough.

Bobby was surprised that something that

should be so simple was turning out to be so hard.

"Why don't we rest for a while?" Bobby suggested.

"Rest? I'm just getting started," Shawn answered with a grin.

Bobby knew why Shawn was smiling. He was good at kicking the ball.

"Boys," Shawn's mother called from the back door. "Come in and have some lemonade. It's hot out there."

"I'm pretty thirsty," Bobby said.

Shawn looked as if he wanted to keep playing. Then he said, "Okay, let's get something to drink."

Mrs. Taylor poured Shawn and Bobby tall glasses of lemonade. The calendar said September, but it still felt like August outside.

Ben, Shawn's younger brother, came into

the kitchen. "I'm bored." He looked at Shawn and Bobby hopefully.

Bobby knew what that meant. Ben wanted to hang out with them.

Shawn shook his head. "We're busy, Ben."

Mrs. Taylor said, "I'm going to the garage to pack some summer things away. It's supposed to get colder this week. I don't want Ben underfoot, so please watch him."

"Mom! Bobby and I are practicing," said Shawn.

"Well, Ben can practice with you," his mother answered.

Shawn looked at her with horror. "No, he can't. He's too little."

"I think you were about Ben's age when you started kicking a soccer ball," Mrs. Taylor reminded Shawn.

Bobby was surprised. That meant Shawn

had been playing around with soccer for a couple of years.

"Where's Sara?" Shawn asked. Sara was Shawn's older sister.

"She's babysitting," his mother told him.

"She should be babysitting for Ben," Shawn muttered.

"I won't be long," Mrs. Taylor said. "Just play upstairs for a while."

Bobby followed Shawn up to his room. Ben tagged along. The first thing Bobby saw in Shawn's room was his soccer gear laid out on his bed. A brown T-shirt. Black soccer shorts. White shoes with spikes. Shin guards.

Bobby had all the same equipment, but it was at the bottom of his closet. He hadn't even taken it out of the bag.

"How come your stuff is on your bed?" Bobby asked.

Shawn shrugged.

"Oh, he likes to look at it. He likes to try on his uniform," Ben said. He stuck his arms up in the air and shouted, "Goal! G-O-A-L."

Ben loved to spell.

Shawn glared at Ben. Bobby walked over to a wire cage on Shawn's desk. Inside the cage, running on a wheel, was Twitch, Shawn's white mouse.

Twitch jumped off the wheel. He came over to Bobby and sniffed at his finger. Then he scampered away.

Bobby noticed a picture on Shawn's desk. "Hey, you've been working on the Worm," he said. The Worm was Planet Man's arch-enemy. Bobby had told Shawn about his art project. Now he and Shawn were planning a comic book about the adventures of Planet Man and the Worm.

Shawn nodded. "I'm not done."

Bobby could see that. Right now, the Worm just looked like, well, a worm. He had a long, squiggly body and two bulging eyes. He didn't look like a villain who could destroy the world.

"Worm. W-O-R-M," Ben said proudly.

"Ben. Stop with the spelling, already," Shawn said.

The phone rang. Ben ran into his parents' bedroom to get it. "H-E-L-L-O," the boys heard him say. Shawn sighed.

Ben came back, holding the phone. "Bobby, it's your mom."

Bobby's mother wanted him at home. "I've gotta go," he told Shawn.

"Too bad," Shawn said. "I wanted to practice some more."

Bobby didn't say anything to that.

When Bobby got home, his parents were waiting for him. They were sitting on the living room couch. Bobby frowned. The Quinn family hardly ever used the living room except when company came.

"Did I do something wrong?" he asked.

"No," his mother replied. "Of course not. We just have something we want to talk to you about."

His parents looked so serious. "Is Lucy okay?" Bobby asked anxiously.

Right then, Lucy bounded into the living room. She looked fine.

"Come sit down, Bobby," his mother said. "We have some big news."

Bobby sat down in the large red chair next to the couch. He liked the red chair. It had plenty of room for Lucy to sit next to him.

He patted the cushion of the chair. That

was all the invitation Lucy needed. She jumped up and snuggled next to Bobby. For once, Lucy was quiet. She wanted to hear the big news, too.

Mr. Quinn cleared his throat. "Bobby, I think you know that your mother and I have wanted to give you a brother or a sister for a while now."

Bobby did know that. His parents talked about how nice it would be to have a baby in the house. Bobby always felt a little funny when they mentioned a new baby. It had been just the three of them for a long time. For his whole life! Now, of course, Lucy made four.

"We thought we would have a baby the way most people do," his mother went on. "But that hasn't happened."

"So we have decided to adopt a baby," his father told him. "You know what adoption means, don't you, Bobby?"

"Sure," Bobby said.

There was a girl in his class who was

adopted. Her name was Jade. Her parents had gone all the way to China to adopt her. Jade had told the class about it in show-and-tell.

"Are you going to China to get a baby? Like Jade?" Bobby asked.

"No," Mrs. Quinn said. "People can go to other countries to adopt babies. But we're going to get ours here."

"Mothers can't always take care of their babies," Mr. Quinn explained to Bobby. "Then they give the baby to an adoption agency, and the agency finds it a good home. We hope the adoption agency will find a baby for us."

Bobby didn't know what to say. This *was* big news.

"When will we get the baby?" he asked.

"We're not sure," his mother answered.

"Sometimes it takes a while. Sometimes babies come right away."

"We've already filled out lots of papers," his father said. "Next, a person from the adoption agency will come to our house. They'll make sure we will be a good family for a baby."

Bobby frowned. "We're a good family. Absolutely. We're a great family."

Lucy gave a short bark. *Of course we're a great family,* she seemed to say.

Mr. and Mrs. Quinn smiled. "I'm glad you and Lucy agree on that," his mother added.

"Will the baby be a boy or a girl?" Bobby asked.

"We don't get to pick," Mrs. Quinn told him. "But we don't care if it's a boy or girl. We just want another child to love."

"You're such a great kid," his father said with a smile. "We know you'll be a wonderful big brother."

"Do you have any more questions?" Mrs. Quinn asked.

Bobby felt as if he had lots more questions. He just wasn't sure what they were yet. He shook his head.

"Well, if you do, ask them. We're all in this together," his father told him.

His mother held her arms out to Bobby. "Come over here and give me a hug."

Bobby gave her a big hug.

"You're a good boy, Bobby," his mother whispered in his ear.

Bobby started to walk to his room. He wanted to think about all this news. Then he did have a question. "Do I have to share my bedroom with the baby?" he asked.

"Oh, no," Mrs. Quinn answered. "Your dad is going to give up his office for the baby's bedroom."

Mr. Quinn frowned. "Well, it might be your sewing room, Jane. We haven't decided yet."

Uh-oh, Bobby thought. He hoped this wasn't going to turn into a fight.

Instead, his parents started laughing. "We'll flip a coin," Mrs. Quinn said. "But don't worry, Bobby. Your room is safe."

When Bobby got upstairs, he flopped on his bed. He stared at the ceiling.

Lucy didn't jump up next to him. She sat on the floor and looked puzzled. Usually Bobby was doing something—drawing, reading, working on the computer, or playing with her. She wasn't used to seeing him doing nothing.

A new baby, Bobby thought. *A brother or a sister.* Wow. He couldn't quite imagine what that would be like.

He thought about the babies he knew. He didn't know many. He remembered his cousins when they were babies. They could be cute. They could also be fussy and stinky.

Bobby looked over at Lucy. She was very cute. She had her stinky moments, too.

"I hope I like this baby as much as I like you, Lucy."

But he didn't really think that was possible.

Kick It!

Bobby looked at himself in the mirror on his closet door.

He was wearing his soccer uniform. Brown shirt, black shorts, long white socks, black sneakers.

Lucy strolled over to him. She looked Bobby up and down. Then she walked away.

"Yeah," Bobby muttered. "I know what you mean."

The shirt was a little snug. The shorts were a little big. The socks looked weird. They went right up to his knees. The shin guards felt stiff and uncomfortable. Only the sneakers seemed okay.

"Bobby!" Mrs. Quinn called from downstairs. "Shawn's here."

Today was the first Saturday soccer practice. Each week there would be two practices, one after school and one on Saturday morning. Soon their team would start playing real games. They would play against other teams from nearby towns. Those games would be on Sunday afternoons.

Bobby walked to his desk. His picture of Planet Man was there. He picked it up. He wanted to draw Planet Man in some new poses. Between soccer practice and homework, he probably wouldn't have time today.

"Bobby!" his mother called again. "Come on! You don't want to be late on your first day."

Bobby put down the picture and grabbed his shin guards. He hadn't tried them on yet. They didn't look very comfortable.

Shawn and his mother were in the kitchen. Mrs. Quinn had Lucy on her leash.

Lucy pranced about. She knew being on her leash meant one thing. She was going outside. And she wanted to go now!

On the way to the park, Bobby and Shawn were quiet.

Bobby was pretty sure they were thinking about the same thing. They would know a few kids on their team, like Candy. But everyone else would be strangers.

Bobby couldn't remember the last time he had met a whole group of kids at one

time. Even though he was sometimes shy with his classmates, they weren't strangers. He had been with many of them since kindergarten.

Lucy had helped Bobby become less shy.

She had helped him make new friends. But he didn't see how Lucy could help him make friends on the soccer field.

As soon as Mrs. Quinn dropped the boys off in the park, they saw Candy. She ran over to them.

"Hi, guys! I wondered where you were. The coach is about to start," she told them.

Before the boys could say anything, Candy went on. "There are seven boys and four girls here. Dexter from our class is one of them. In this league, we play with seven kids on the field." Candy counted on her fingers. She wasn't very good at math. "That means four kids will sit out at every game. Of course, that doesn't mean for the whole game. The coach can take players in and out—"

A shrill whistle blast stopped Candy in the middle of her sentence.

"We better get going," Bobby said.

Shawn and Candy hurried toward the field. Bobby lagged behind.

Coach Morris blew on his whistle once more. "Team! When you hear this whistle you stop what you're doing. You look at me."

All the kids looked at him.

"We are here to play soccer," he told them. "We will practice hard. That will turn us into a good team. Then we will play hard."

Some of the kids were nodding. Shawn was one of them.

"Now we are going to introduce ourselves. I'm Coach Morris." He pointed at Candy. "Say your name."

"I'm Candy. I've never played soccer before but—"

"Your name is enough," the coach said in a firm voice. "Next." He looked at Shawn.

Shawn said his name so quietly Bobby could barely hear him.

"Juan?" the coach asked.

"No. Shawn," he said more loudly.

"All right, you're Shawn," Coach Morris said. "Let's all try to speak up."

Bobby said his name. He tried to speak up.

Pretty soon, everyone had given their names. Bobby tried to remember who was who, but only a few names stuck in his head.

"The next thing we are going to do is pick a name for our team," Coach Morris told the group. "We need something that goes with the color of our shirts. What's brown?" he asked.

"Mud's brown," Candy said.

The coach frowned at Candy. "Do you think the Mud is a good name for our team?"

Candy looked embarrassed.

Bobby and Shawn glanced at each other. Candy almost never got embarrassed.

A boy named Tim said, "Bear cubs are brown. Like the Chicago Cubs."

Tim must be a Cubs fan, too, Bobby thought.

"Yes," the coach agreed. "Cubs are brown, but they are not very fast, are they? In soccer you want to be fast. Anybody else?"

Nobody said anything for a few minutes. Finally a girl named Jane said, "Maybe cubs aren't fast, but some bears are. I did a report on them in school."

"Bears." Coach Morris thought about that. "Well, bears at least seem tough. Let's take a vote. How many of you like the name Bears?"

The kids looked around at each other. Slowly, most of them raised their hands.

Nobody seemed to have a better suggestion.

"Okay, then. We are the Bears," the coach said. "Now comes the most important question. How many of you have played soccer before?"

Bobby was worried. He was afraid that he and Candy might be the only ones who had never played. It made him feel better when only about half the kids raised their hands.

It didn't seem to make Coach Morris feel better. He shook his head.

"Okay, I guess I better start at the beginning," the coach said. "Even though some of you know how to play, I want you to listen up anyway. There are some things you might have forgotten."

The coach took them over to the field. It was a large rectangle, with a circle in the middle and a goal at either end.

"The most important skill you need to play soccer is good kicking," Coach Morris said in a booming voice. "Kicking is what moves the ball from one player to the next. And kicking is how you score goals."

Coach Morris stood in the middle of the field and showed the group the proper way to kick. He picked up a soccer ball and kicked it hard. It went almost as far as the goal.

"You've gotta practice your kicking," he said. "Make a target and try to kick to it. Practice kicking the ball with your friends."

Bobby thought kicking the ball correctly looked plenty hard. But there was more. Much more.

"You also have to learn how to pass the ball to another player. That's how we move the ball down the field." Coach Morris looked around at his team. “You,” he said, pointing to Shawn. “Come here. We’ll pass the ball back and forth between us.”

Bobby was glad the coach hadn’t picked him to pass the ball. Shawn didn’t look nervous. Not very nervous, anyway.

“This is how you pass a ball,” the coach said. He showed them how to use the flat,

inside part of the foot. "You can control the ball this way."

Raising his foot and swinging it forward, the coach passed the ball to Shawn. When the ball came to him, Shawn used his foot to pass the ball back. They passed the ball between them a few times.

“Not bad,” Coach Morris told Shawn. Shawn grinned.

By the time Coach Morris had explained a few more rules and showed them what to do if they were protecting the goal, Bobby’s head was swimming.

“I’ve got some booklets to hand out after practice,” Coach Morris said. “I want you to study them. They explain more about the rules of the game.”

Bobby looked over to the sidelines where his mother was waiting. Maybe it was time to go home.

Mrs. Quinn was sitting on a park bench. She was talking to one of the other mothers. She didn’t seem to be paying much attention to Bobby’s soccer team.

Lucy *was* very interested in what was happening on the field. She was tugging on her leash. When Bobby waved at her, Lucy gave several short barks.

"Bobby!" Coach Morris was staring straight at him. "Can we have your attention, please?"

Now it was Bobby's turn to be embarrassed.

"As I was saying," Coach Morris went on, "we're going to spend some time running up and down the field. We will divide into two teams. One team will try to kick the ball down the field. The other team will try to steal the ball. Then it will be their turn to kick it up the field."

Soon the players were ready. The black-and-white soccer ball was placed in the circle in the middle of the field. The coach blew his whistle.

Kickoff!

Dexter kicked the ball. Other kids kicked

it, too. Bobby didn't come close to putting his foot on the ball. But still he ran. Up the field. Down the field.

Suddenly, out of the corner of his eye, Bobby saw something. Something running fast across the field. Something that could bark.

"Lucy!" Bobby yelled. "Go back."

Lucy glanced at Bobby. Her leash was flapping behind her. That didn't matter. She kept running.

Now the other kids on the soccer team noticed Lucy. They kept kicking the ball. But they were laughing and pointing, too.

Lucy gave a sharp bark. She had spotted the ball! Lucy loved to chase balls. She cut across the field in front of some of the kids. She got closer and closer to the ball. Then, when she was right on top of it, Lucy pushed

the ball hard with her nose. She caught up with it, and pushed it again. Really hard. It went right past the goal line!

"Hey, hey!" Coach Morris shouted. "Where did that dog come from?"

The kids were laughing and cheering. Lucy finally stopped running. She sat on her haunches, panting. She looked very happy.

Bobby was not happy. *Uh-oh,* he thought. Wait until the coach found out that Lucy belonged to him. "She's mine," he squeaked.

Mrs. Quinn hurried up to the huddle. "I'm so sorry. Lucy is our dog. She got away from me." She frowned at Lucy as she grabbed her leash.

The coach shook his head. "She's a wild one," he said. "But she sure is fast."

"Hey," Dexter said. "Lucy is brown. Why don't we call our team the Beagles? You said we should name it after a fast animal."

For the first time all afternoon, Coach Morris cracked a smile. "The Beagles, huh? What do the rest of you think? Raise your hand if you like the name Beagles."

Everyone liked the idea. Dexter clapped Bobby on the shoulder. "We're naming the team after your dog."

Bobby was happy now. It was always the same. Everyone loved Lucy.

The Baby Lady

Once again, Lucy was helping him make new friends. The boys and girls on the soccer team were excited about calling their team the Beagles. When practice was over, everyone wanted to pat Lucy.

Lucy loved all the attention.

That was the best part of practice. But Lucy wasn't at the next practice. Bobby was on his own. His kicking wasn't very good.

Not very good at all. He was happy when practice was over. But soon he'd have to go back on the soccer field again. Was he looking forward to it? Absolutely not!

There *was* something Bobby was excited about. Planet Man! He was eager to get home after practice and start drawing.

When Bobby got home, however, he could see right away there wouldn't be time for drawing.

The first thing he smelled when he opened the door was furniture polish. The first thing he saw was a vase of flowers in the living room. The first thing he heard was the vacuum cleaner.

Something was up. The house was never this clean unless company was coming.

"Mom?" Bobby yelled. He tried to make his voice heard over the noisy machine.

The noise stopped. Mrs. Quinn came into the living room. She looked frazzled.

"What's going on?" Bobby asked.

"A woman from the adoption agency is coming over in a few minutes. She wants to see our home."

"Did you know she was coming?" Bobby asked.

Mrs. Quinn shook her head. "The agency called about an hour ago. The visit is supposed to be a surprise. That way they can see how we really live."

"This looks better than how we really live," Bobby noted.

His mother finally smiled. "Well, just a little better, maybe. Now I'm going upstairs to comb my hair and put on some lipstick. If the agency worker arrives, let her in and talk to her until I come down."

Bobby sat on the couch. He waited nervously for the doorbell to ring. What was he supposed to say to this woman?

Just then, something caught his eye. Lucy was creeping out of the front closet. She must have been hiding in there from the vacuum cleaner. She hated that noise.

"Lucy, come here, girl," Bobby called.

Lucy slunk over to Bobby. She looked around. He could almost hear her thinking, *Is that awful noise gone for good?*

"It's okay," Bobby said, patting her. Then the doorbell rang. Not once. Several times.

The chimes of the bell set Lucy off. She began to bark. *BARK!*

"Lucy, quiet!" Bobby yelled.

That stopped Lucy for about two seconds. Then the bell rang again. The barking started again.

Bobby ran to the door. Lucy ran behind him, still barking.

He flung the door open. A lady with dark hair, wearing a blue raincoat and blue gloves, stood in the doorway.

Lucy jumped on her.

"Down, Lucy!" Bobby pulled her away from the visitor. "Hello," he said.

"Hello." The lady said her name, but Bobby didn't catch it. Lucy's barking was too loud.

"May I come in?" the woman said. "I think your mother is expecting me."

"Lucy, settle down!" Now Lucy added her prancy dance to her barking. "Yes, she is," Bobby said, opening the door wider.

Mrs. Quinn was hurrying down the stairs. "Oh, hello," she greeted the woman. "I see you met my son, Bobby. And our dog, Lucy."

Lucy was finally quiet. She looked over the visitor with a curious expression.

"Uh, yes." The woman frowned. "We've met."

Mrs. Quinn said, "Let me take your coat. Then I'll show you around. Bobby, why don't you stay down here." His mother gave him a look. "With Lucy."

Bobby knew what that look meant. He was supposed to keep Lucy quiet.

"Come on, Lucy." Bobby led her into the den. His mother kept paper and colored pencils for him there. Maybe he could do a few sketches of Planet Man.

For a while Lucy sat near Bobby as he drew. Finally Lucy got bored and wandered off. Bobby didn't notice.

He was still hard at work when his mother and the adoption agency woman came downstairs. Since he hadn't heard her name, Bobby thought of her as the Baby Lady.

The Baby Lady and Mrs. Quinn walked into the den.

"What are you drawing?" the Baby Lady asked.

Bobby didn't really like people looking at his artwork until he was finished. He pulled the paper closer to him. "A picture to help save the environment."

"My, that's an ambitious project," the Baby Lady said.

"Yes, it is," Bobby answered politely.

"I take it you like to draw?" the Baby Lady asked.

"Yes," Bobby agreed.

"He's a very good artist," Mrs. Quinn said.

"What else do you like to do in your free time, Bobby?" the Baby Lady asked.

Before Bobby could answer, Lucy trotted into the room. She had something in her mouth.

"What have you got there, Lucy?" Mrs. Quinn asked.

Mrs. Quinn tried to pull the thing from her mouth.

Lucy pulled it right back. She thought it was a game!

"Come on, Lucy," Mrs. Quinn demanded.

Lucy dropped a chewed-up ball of blue leather on the floor. Mrs. Quinn picked it up and examined it. "I think it's a glove."

The Baby Lady took it from her. "I think it's my glove."

All eyes turned to Lucy.

"Lucy!" Mrs. Quinn said sharply.

Lucy wasn't just cute. She was smart. She knew she had done something wrong.

"Oh, I'm so, so sorry," Mrs. Quinn said to the Baby Lady.

"I'm sorry, too," Bobby whispered.

Lucy hung her head. She seemed sorry as well.

"We will replace your gloves, of course," Mrs. Quinn added.

The Baby Lady shook her head. "It's all right. They didn't cost much. Dogs will be dogs, I guess."

The Baby Lady didn't seem to be mad. But she didn't seem pleased, either.

Mrs. Quinn walked the Baby Lady to the front door and said goodbye. Then she came back to the den. She sat down in a chair. She put her hand to her head.

"Do you have a headache, Mom?" Bobby asked.

"I've got one now." Mrs. Quinn turned to Lucy. "How could you, Lucy?"

Lucy tried to look busy rolling around on the floor.

"Does this mean we won't get a baby?" Bobby asked anxiously.

He still wasn't sure how he felt about a new baby coming, but he didn't want his parents to miss out on one just because of Lucy.

"I don't think a chewed glove ruins our

chances," Mrs. Quinn said. "But it sure was embarrassing."

Bobby nodded. Even he had been embarrassed.

"Lucy can't be acting up like this when the new baby comes," Mrs. Quinn said. "She has to settle down. She needs to go back to obedience school."

Bobby thought about all the things that came with babies. Diapers, booties, blankets, stuffed animals. Lots of things for Lucy to chew. Plus, babies liked to sleep. Lucy liked to bark.

His parents were ready for a new baby. Maybe he was, too. But Lucy wasn't.

5 Practice

Mrs. Quinn called the park district about obedience class just a few minutes after the Baby Lady left.

Lucy had taken a group class at the park district over the summer. The teacher's name was Wendy.

When Mrs. Quinn got off the phone, she said, "Lucy is registered for a private obedience class. It will be right after your soccer practice. But Wendy isn't working at the park district anymore. Lucy will have a new teacher. Mr. Morris."

That got Bobby's attention. "You mean Coach Morris?"

Mrs. Quinn said, "Yes, I suppose so."

"But how can Coach Morris also be Mr. Morris the dog trainer?" Bobby asked.

"Well," Mrs. Quinn replied, "he works for the park district. Maybe he does several different jobs for them."

Bobby looked at Lucy. He felt sorry for her. Coach Morris was very strict on the soccer field. He would probably be just as strict when it came to teaching a dog how to behave.

Sure enough, the next practice was no picnic. There was the usual drill. Kicking practice. Passing practice. Trying-to-steal-the-ball practice.

When it was over, the coach blew his whistle. "Gather round, everybody. I want to talk to you."

Talking! That sounded great to Bobby. Much better than running.

The team sat in a circle on the grass in front of Coach Morris.

"Tomorrow is our first game," Coach Morris began. He looked down at a card he held in his hand. "It's against the Plainfield Rockets."

"I have a cousin on that team," Candy said brightly. "He said they're really good."

The coach frowned at her for interrupting. "Now, we've done a lot of practicing on the basics, but that's different from playing a real game. A real game is tough."

Bobby felt a knot in the pit of his stomach. He was sure that was true.

The coach continued. "Tomorrow, I am going to pick seven of you to start the game. One of you will be the goalkeeper."

Bobby hoped it wouldn't be him. The goalie tried to prevent the other team from scoring points. He could try to keep the ball out of the goal with his feet. He could use his hands as well. Bobby didn't like the idea of the ball coming right at him. And if the ball got past him, well, that was bad. One point for the other team. If the Plainfield Rockets got more points, they would win.

No, Bobby didn't want to be the goalkeeper. Absolutely not.

Coach Morris talked more about the next day's game. Bobby's attention wandered. He was thinking about Planet Man. His art teacher said the best pictures would be hung on the school wall. He hoped his was good enough.

"So, does everyone understand?" the coach asked.

Bobby looked around. His teammates were nodding. Bobby wondered what he had missed.

"So I will see you here for our game at twelve sharp," Coach Morris said.

The Beagles got up to leave. Bobby saw his mother coming toward him. Lucy was on her leash, pulling her forward. It was time for obedience class. Poor Lucy. She didn't know what she was in for.

Bobby leaned down to give frisky Lucy a pat. "Hi," he said.

Coach Morris walked over to them. He greeted Mrs. Quinn. "So, I understand I'm going to be working with your dog."

"This is Lucy," Mrs. Quinn said.

Coach Morris replied, "Yes, I remember Lucy."

Bobby couldn't tell how he felt about

that. "Can I go sit on the bench?" he asked his mother. All that running around had tired him out.

But before she could answer, Coach Morris said, "Oh, no, Bobby. You are going to be a part of this training. A big part."

Bobby had worked with Lucy during her last obedience classes, but he'd thought maybe he would get a pass today.

"Lucy is your dog, isn't she?" the coach asked Bobby.

Bobby nodded.

"Then you have to know how to control her," Coach Morris said.

Bobby thought, *I don't want to control Lucy. I just want to have fun with her.*

Coach Morris must have read his mind because he said, "Dogs like to have fun, but they like to know someone is in charge, too."

He turned to Mrs. Quinn. "What are Lucy's biggest problems?"

"She barks," Mrs. Quinn said with a sigh. "She chews things. She jumps on visitors."

Lucy looked as if she would like to jump on the coach right now.

Coach Morris said, "Let me explain something to you. Dogs are pack animals. That means they like to have a leader. Out in the wild, a pack of dogs always had a leader. Our dogs want the humans in their lives to be their pack leaders. Otherwise, they will make up their own rules."

"Well, Lucy has definitely been making her own rules lately," Mrs. Quinn said, shaking her head.

"A beagle like Lucy needs lots of exercise. Is she getting it?" Coach Morris asked.

"Maybe not enough," Mrs. Quinn admitted.

"She needs her own chew toys so she doesn't chew shoes," the coach said.

Or gloves, Bobby thought.

"She also must learn the meaning of the word 'no,'" Coach Morris added. "We'll make sure she learns it."

Bobby frowned. Coach Morris sounded even more stern than he did on the soccer field. Mrs. Quinn seemed a little surprised by his serious tone, too.

Before she could say anything, the coach said, "Let's start Lucy's lesson."

The next hour was an eye-opener for Bobby. Usually Lucy didn't listen much to anyone. Not his mother. Not his father. Certainly not him. She had a mind of her own.

But right from the first, she paid attention to Coach Morris. Maybe it was the way he stood, as if he was in charge. Maybe it was the firmness in his voice. Either way, when he told Lucy to sit or stop barking, she looked up at him for a moment and did what she was told.

Then Coach Morris said, "Now you two are going to try to control Lucy. It's important that each of you learns to be a pack leader, the one in charge."

Bobby and his mother exchanged glances. It was one thing for Coach Morris to look like a leader—he *was* a leader. But Lucy knew from experience that she could get almost anything from her owners if she looked cute enough—or if she barked long enough.

The lesson ended with Bobby and his mother learning how to act like leaders. They stood tall. They tried to imitate the strength Coach Morris had in his voice.

Lucy looked confused at first. *Who are you people?* she seemed to say. *Let's play!*

Bobby and Mrs. Quinn stayed firm. Only after Lucy had shown good behavior were they allowed to hug her or give her one of the treats Coach Morris had in his pocket.

"I hope the next time we meet, Mr. Quinn will be with us," Coach Morris said. "I like to have the whole family involved when it comes to training a dog. Every member of the family needs to know how to work with its pet."

"I'll see that he's here," Mrs. Quinn said meekly.

Wow, Bobby thought. It seemed Coach Morris knew how to be the boss over everyone. Even his mom.

6
First Game

Bobby and his mother came home after Lucy's lesson. They told Mr. Quinn all about it. He looked impressed.

"Coach Morris said you are going to have to get more involved, too," Mrs. Quinn told her husband. "Maybe you could take Lucy out for a walk now and then. You both could use the exercise."

When Bobby got up the next morning,

his father was coming into the house after walking Lucy. Mr. Quinn usually did what his wife asked.

"Lucy and I just spent some quality time together," he said, smiling.

Lucy jumped on the sofa and curled up. It seemed like the walk had tired her out.

"Down, Lucy," Mr. Quinn said.

Lucy just looked at him.

"Down," Mr. Quinn repeated.

Lucy rolled over and scratched herself.

Mrs. Quinn came into the room. "Down!" she said in her best pack-leader voice.

Lucy didn't look happy about it, but she did get off the sofa. She walked out of the room, her tail high.

"How did you do that?" Mr. Quinn asked his wife.

"I guess I'm just more of a pack leader

than you are," Mrs. Quinn said with a smile.

Mr. Quinn shook his head and followed Lucy out of the room.

"Bobby," his mother said, "Shawn called. He wanted to know if you could come over and practice before the game."

Bobby shrugged. He took Lucy's place on the sofa.

Mrs. Quinn sat next to him. "I take it you don't feel like practicing," she said.

Bobby shook his head. "I'd rather work on my Planet Man picture. I thought Shawn might want to work on our comic book. I asked him yesterday, but he never gave me an answer one way or the other. . . ." Bobby's voice trailed off.

"Shawn's mother told me how much he liked soccer when he played last year," Mrs. Quinn said.

"He likes it this year, too," Bobby said glumly.

"And you don't?" his mother asked.

"It's okay," Bobby said.

Mrs. Quinn patted his hair. "You haven't even played one game yet, Bobby. All you've done is go to practice sessions. It might still turn out to be fun."

Bobby thought about his mother's words while he was putting on his uniform. Soccer didn't feel like fun. It felt more like taking a test. A real soccer game? That felt like a really big test.

Lots of people were at the park when Bobby and his parents arrived. Some people were sitting on the sidelines in folding chairs they had brought from home. Others were walking up and down the field.

"The nice weather has certainly brought

out a crowd," Mr. Quinn commented.

"I think every single player on both teams must have someone here," Mrs. Quinn added.

Too many people, Bobby thought. He felt as if a soccer ball was rolling around in his stomach.

Coach Morris blew a long blast on his whistle.

Mr. Quinn gave Bobby's shoulder a pat. "I think your coach is trying to get the Beagles together."

Bobby slowly walked over and joined his teammates.

"Hey, Bobby, where's Lucy?" Candy asked. "She should be here. She's our team mascot, after all."

"Lucy's not ready to be here yet," Coach Morris answered for Bobby. "She needs to learn how to control herself first. A game would get her too excited."

Once all the team had gathered, Coach Morris began his pep talk. "I know this is your first game. But I expect to see good offense and defense out there."

He called out several names, including Dexter's and Tim's. The coach told those kids they would be forwards, the players in charge of moving the ball toward the Rockets' goal. Bobby was one of the defenders. He would help keep the ball away from the Beagles' goal. Coach Morris picked Candy to be the goalkeeper.

Bobby looked at Candy. Even she seemed a little worried about having such an important position.

Coach Morris sent Dexter out with one of the Rockets for the coin toss. The kids who knew a lot about soccer called Dexter the striker. That meant he was the best kicker on the team.

Heads! The Beagles won the toss. Coach Morris told Dexter to kick off.

Dexter didn't try to kick the ball too far. Coach Morris had told them the idea was to keep control of the ball and move it down the field. Dexter and a couple of the other kids passed the ball back and forth toward the Rockets' goal. They didn't do too well. One of the Rockets stole the ball away.

Now it was time for Bobby and the other defenders to stop the Rockets.

That didn't happen. With one long kick, a Rocket put the ball inside the Beagles' goal. Candy just watched it whiz by. Her mouth formed a big round O.

That was the way the game went for the first half. The Rockets had the ball most of the time. They made another goal. Bobby ran up and down the field, but he never came close to having his foot on the ball.

At halftime the score was Rockets 2, Beagles 0.

Coach Morris said, "We're two behind. But we can catch up. I want to see more kicking. Defenders, you were letting the Rockets control the field. I'm going to shake things up in the second half. Offensive players, except for Dexter, you go on defense. Defense, now you're offense."

Bobby was now an offensive player. He sighed. Trying to make a goal seemed even harder than playing defense.

As it turned out, it didn't seem to matter if he was playing offense or defense. Once again, he didn't get anywhere near the ball during the second half of the game.

Shawn kicked the ball to get it down the

field. Then he passed it to Dexter. Dexter made one hard kick. Goal!

The game finally ended. The Rockets won, 2 to 1.

All Bobby got for his effort was a lot of sweat and tired legs.

Coach Morris didn't look too mad when the team gathered after the game.

"Beagles, we've got a lot of work to do." He took off his cap and rubbed his fingers through his gray hair. "Our passing isn't great. Except for Dexter, our shooting isn't much, either. Candy, you did okay as goalie. But next time, I'm going to give someone else the chance to play that position."

Coach Morris looked around the circle.

Bobby put his head down. The chance to play goalkeeper? The coach made it seem like a prize. Who wanted a prize like that?

Second Game

The Beagles' second game didn't go much better than the first.

This time they played a team called the Wasps. Their sting was pretty sharp.

With ten minutes left in the game, Coach Morris said, "Bobby Quinn, I want you in as goalie. Stop those Wasps!"

It was the longest ten minutes of Bobby's life. He stood at the goal line hoping the ball would not come to him. One time, it did come close. Good thing Shawn stole the ball away from the Wasp who was moving it toward the goal.

Bobby gave a sigh of relief. He was even happier when the game ended.

The score was the same as the game against the Rockets—2 to 1. Wasps win.

Coach Morris gave the team a talking-to. He told the Beagles everything they had done wrong. It took him a while to finish.

"We're going to practice harder next week. And I want you to practice at home. That's the only way this team is going to become winners," Coach Morris told them.

During the week, Bobby tried to forget about soccer. On Wednesday, he missed midweek practice. He was home sick with a sore throat. He stayed home from school on

Thursday, too. By Friday he was fine. He was glad to go back to school. He didn't want to miss art class. He wanted to show Miss Olson, the art teacher, his picture of Planet Man.

Miss Olson told the children they should draw their picture in pencil first. Then they could go on to markers or paint.

Bobby was very glad to be working in pencil. He needed to do a lot of erasing. His picture was of Planet Man on a horse, chasing two men who were dumping garbage in a river. Drawing Planet Man was easy. Drawing the horse was hard. The horse looked as if it had a mattress for a body and sticks for legs.

"I'm going to keep working on my horse," he told Miss Olson when he showed her the sketch.

"Yes, the horse needs work," Miss Olson agreed. "Everything else is very good. Take some horse books out of the library. Trace the horses on paper. Then practice drawing your own horses."

"I'll do that," Bobby said. He was eager to get started.

On Saturday, Bobby and his parents went

to the park early with Lucy for her obedience lesson. Today, Lucy's lesson had been changed to before soccer practice. Lucy seemed eager to get started. That surprised Bobby.

"Lucy likes her training," Bobby whispered to his father.

Coach Morris heard him. "She feels comfortable. You must be practicing with her."

"We are," Mrs. Quinn agreed. "Lucy seems to understand that we're the ones in charge."

"And she's a happier dog for it, isn't she?" the coach asked.

Bobby had to admit it was true. Lucy didn't fuss as much as she used to. She wasn't bored, because they kept her busy. She seemed much calmer. That meant fewer chewed socks and shoes. Not so much howling.

"I think Lucy will need only a few more lessons," Coach Morris said. "She's got the idea now."

"Lucy!" Mrs. Quinn said. "Good for you!"

Mr. Quinn patted Lucy on the head.

Lucy stood tall, her tail up. She seemed to know she was a good student.

"Good for all of you," Coach Morris said. "This is what happens when you work hard as a team."

Coach Morris seemed to be looking right at Bobby. And he seemed to be talking about more than Lucy.

After Lucy's lesson, it was time for the Beagles' practice session. *Maybe the coach is right,* Bobby thought. *Maybe I should work more at soccer.* During practice, he paid attention to the coach's directions. He tried harder to kick the ball, and he did manage to kick it a few times. Even when Coach Morris made him practice as goalie, Bobby gave it his best effort.

Coach Morris noticed. "You're trying, Bobby."

"Thanks," Bobby replied. He didn't think he was getting much better. But at least he was giving it his best shot.

Sunday morning, Bobby woke up to the sound of rain, a hard, driving rain beating against the window. There was a sharp clap of thunder. Lucy jumped up on Bobby's bed.

"Don't be scared," Bobby said, giving Lucy a hug. He didn't like thunder, either, but he wanted to show Lucy he was brave.

The rain had lightened a little by the time Bobby came downstairs for breakfast. His father was making what he called "the best oatmeal ever!"

Every time Mr. Quinn said that, Bobby replied, "There's no such thing as the best oatmeal because all oatmeal is bad."

"Nonsense, Bobby," Mr. Quinn said, putting a steaming bowl in front of him. "Oatmeal is good and good for you."

Bobby looked down at his oatmeal. Maybe it wasn't his favorite food, but at least his father loaded it up with brown sugar and berries.

"Where's Mom?" Bobby asked.

"She went to get a few things at the store," Mr. Quinn told him.

Just then, Mrs. Quinn hurried in from outside. She shook off a few drops. "It's still raining," she said.

Bobby looked out the window. It was dark, and wet, and chilly. The last thing he wanted to do was play soccer this afternoon.

After breakfast, his father started a fire in the fireplace. Bobby gathered the horse books he had taken from the library and a pad and pencil. Then he flopped down on the floor. Lucy flopped next to him. Bobby looked at horse pictures and started to draw. He looked a little more. He drew a little more.

He must have drawn for a long time.

"Bobby," his mother said from the doorway, "it's time to get ready for soccer."

Bobby barely looked up. "Oh, I'm not going today."

His mother frowned. "What do you mean? Are you feeling sick again?"

Bobby sat up. "No, I'm fine."

"Then why do you think you're not going?" Mrs. Quinn asked.

"I want to stay home. I need to finish my

drawing of Planet Man." Bobby held up his latest sketch.

Mr. Quinn came into the room.

"Bobby doesn't want to go to soccer," Mrs. Quinn informed him. "He wants to stay home and draw."

Bobby's parents were both frowning.

"Anyway, it's raining out," Bobby explained. "And it's cold." He didn't see what was wrong with skipping the game.

"Bobby," his father began, "you can't miss a game just because there's something else you would rather do."

"Why not?" Bobby asked, surprised.

"When you joined the team, you made a commitment," Mrs. Quinn said. "Do you know what a commitment is?"

"Not exactly," Bobby answered.

"It's like a promise," his mother told him.

"You agreed to be a team member and be there for the games."

Now it was Bobby's turn to frown. "They don't need me. I'm not that good."

"You're getting better," Mr. Quinn said. "The coach said so at practice."

"Besides," Mrs. Quinn said, "what if two, or three, or four kids on the team decided they didn't want to play because it's raining?"

Bobby thought about it for a moment. "I guess we would have to forfeit the game."

"That's right," Mr. Quinn said. "You're on a team. You have to do what's best for the team. You can't just think of yourself."

Bobby would have liked to think only about himself. Then he could stay in his nice warm house, drawing. But he was a Beagle. The team was even named after his dog.

"I'll get ready," Bobby said.

Lucy had been sitting quietly. Now she gave a big, long stretch. She looked around. Bobby knew what that meant. She wanted to go for a walk.

Bobby added, “Can we take Lucy to the game today? She could use the exercise.”

Mrs. Quinn smiled. “That’s a good idea. We can test out her training. If she gets antsy, Dad can walk around the park with her.” She added, “I’m proud of you, Bobby. Now you’re thinking about the team *and* Lucy.”

By the time they got to the soccer field, it had stopped raining. It was still cold. Bobby had to wear a sweater under his jersey. It felt bulky and uncomfortable, but he was warm.

Coach Morris blew his whistle. The Beagles gathered around him.

“Team, I like what I’ve been seeing at practice. I think we’re going to do well today.

The team we're playing is the Wizards, but *we're* the ones who are going to make magic."

Then the coach assigned the positions. "Bobby Quinn. Goalkeeper."

Bobby had never started a game as the goalie. He wondered if this meant he was going to have to play the position for both halves. He looked at the sidelines. Lucy was running in small circles. That was the way his stomach felt.

After the coin toss, Bobby took his position in front of the goal line. He waited and watched.

"Keep your eye on the ball!" his father yelled.

He would try.

For the first few minutes of the game, all the action was on the other side of the field. The Beagles were trying to score. No one could quite kick it in. Then, suddenly, a foot got on the ball. It made a short, hard kick. Goal for the Beagles!

There were so many kids huddled near the goal, Bobby couldn't quite see who had made the kick. Was it Dexter? Shawn? Then he saw Candy jumping up and down. Candy had scored!

This made Bobby feel good. He was happy for Candy. He also knew that Candy wasn't a very good player. If she could make a goal, maybe he could stop one.

His chance came later in the half. One of the Wizards, a big, stocky boy, was pushing the ball down the field. None of the Beagles could get the ball away from him. The Wizard kept the ball moving. Then he gave it a big kick. Bobby could see the ball coming right at him.

Uh-oh!

The ball was flying through the air. It was high enough to swat with his hands. Could he do it? Bobby forgot he was nervous. He stepped toward the ball and hit it hard.

The ball fell back onto the field. Bobby had stopped it. No goal for the Wizards this time!

Bobby was breathing hard. He looked over at the sidelines. His parents were clapping. Lucy was barking. Even Coach Morris was smiling.

Bobby smiled, too. He had paid attention. He had tried his best. He had stopped the Wizards in their tracks!

Wow, Bobby thought. *Maybe soccer is fun after all.*

8 Three Beagles

Shawn and Bobby got off the school bus.

"We don't have any homework today," Shawn said. "Let's do something before dinner."

"Soccer?" Bobby asked. "You could kick, and I could practice being goalkeeper."

"I was thinking we could work on Planet Man and the Worm," Shawn said.

Both boys started to laugh.

"This is a switch," Bobby said.

"It sure is," agreed Shawn. "Maybe we can play a little *and* draw a little."

Bobby nodded. "Come over as soon as you can."

A happy Bobby opened the door to his house. But when he saw who was sitting on the couch, he felt odd. It was the Baby Lady. Did this mean the baby had arrived?

"We have a visitor," Mrs. Quinn said.

Bobby came into the living room. He noticed that Lucy was quietly stretched out next to the coffee table. "Hello," he whispered.

"You remember Mrs. Brady?" his mother asked.

He nodded. *So that's her name,* Bobby thought. Then he looked around. "Where is he?" he asked.

Mrs. Quinn looked puzzled.

"Or she," Bobby added.

Mrs. Brady laughed. "He means the baby."

Now it was Mrs. Quinn's turn to smile. "Oh, Mrs. Brady is just here for another visit. It will still be a while before we get a baby."

Bobby wasn't sure if he felt glad or sad about that. He was looking forward to a brother or sister. But maybe not quite yet.

"Come sit down, Bobby," Mrs. Quinn said.

Bobby sat in the big red chair. As soon as Lucy saw that, she jumped up on the chair with him. But she didn't do it in a wild way. She didn't bark or howl. She neatly hopped up and snuggled beside Bobby.

"Lucy seems much quieter than the last time I saw her," Mrs. Brady noted.

"We've been taking her to obedience classes," Mrs. Quinn said. "No more chewed gloves."

Bobby thought his mother still looked embarrassed about that.

"Well, how wonderful," replied Mrs. Brady. "I understand dogs can make a lot of progress with a good teacher."

"Mr. Morris is both Lucy's teacher and Bobby's soccer coach," Mrs. Quinn said.

Mrs. Brady turned to Bobby. "You're on a soccer team?" When Bobby nodded, she asked, "What's the name of your team?"

"The Beagles," Bobby replied.

Mrs. Brady looked confused for a moment. "Beagles? Like Lucy?"

"The team saw how fast Lucy could run, and they decided they wanted to be Beagles, too!" Bobby said proudly.

Lucy gave a little bark at that. But it was a nice, polite bark.

There was a knock on the door. "That's

Shawn. We're going to play for a while," Bobby said.

"Have fun," Mrs. Quinn told him.

Bobby hopped off the chair, and Lucy followed him.

"Goodbye," Bobby called to Mrs. Brady.

Shawn was standing outside, his soccer ball in his hand. Bobby and Shawn went around to the backyard with Lucy trotting behind.

"Let's kick it around for a while," Shawn said. He put the ball down and gave it a long kick.

Bobby was about to chase it down, but Lucy got there first. When she reached the ball, she pushed it with her nose. Then Lucy turned and looked at them. *C'mon, you guys,* she seemed to say.

Bobby and Shawn started laughing.

Lucy nudged the ball again. Then she danced around it.

Bobby ran over to the ball and kicked it toward Shawn. Lucy ran after it once more.

"Lucy's a real Beagle," Shawn said.

"She likes soccer," Bobby agreed. "And you know what? So do I!"

Read all the books about Bobby and Lucy!

Absolutely Lucy

Bobby's mother smiled. "Now it's time for your special present," she said.

His father said, "Close your eyes."

Bobby was glad to close his eyes. It would be easier to look surprised when he opened them.

"Okay, Bobby," his father called, "you can look!"

Bobby opened his eyes. He didn't have to pretend to be surprised. Or happy. In his father's arms was a puppy. The cutest, squirmiest little dog Bobby had ever seen.

Lucy on the Loose

"Ben!" Shawn said. "What happened to Lucy?"

"She . . . she ran away!" Ben said in a shaky voice.

Bobby jumped up. "Ran away? Where?"

"That way." Ben was confused. He pointed in one direction. "Or maybe that way." He pointed in the other direction.

"Which way was it?" Shawn demanded.

"I'm not sure." Ben was almost crying. "But she was chasing a big orange C-A-T!"

Look at Lucy!

On the way out, a large, colorful poster taller than the boys caught Bobby's eye.

The poster had a drawing of different kinds of animals crowded together in front of a television camera. Across the top were the words WANTED: SPOKESPET FOR PET-O-RAMA! Under the picture of the animals it said, "Is your pet cute? Smart? Funny? Enter the Pet-O-Rama spokespet contest and your pet could be on TV!"

Bobby read the poster carefully. Cute, smart, funny? That described Lucy! She could win the spokespet contest, easy!